RAINBOW
magic ®

The Fun Day Fairies

For Plum Tilley, with lots of
love and fairy magic

Special thanks to
Sue Mongredien

ORCHARD BOOKS
338 Euston Road, London NW1 3BH
Orchard Books Australia
Level 17/207 Kent Street, Sydney, NSW 2000
A Paperback Original

First published in Great Britain in 2006

© 2009 Rainbow Magic Limited.
A HIT Entertainment company. Rainbow Magic
is a trademark of Rainbow Magic Limited.
Reg. U.S. Pat. & Tm. Off. And other countries.

HiT entertainment

Illustrations © Georgie Ripper 2006

A CIP catalogue record for this book is available
from the British Library.

ISBN 978 1 84616 193 3
7 9 10 8 6

Printed in Great Britain

Orchard Books is a division of Hachette Children's Books,
an Hachette UK company

www.hachette.co.uk

Sienna

the Saturday

Fairy

by Daisy Meadows

illustrated by Georgie Ripper

ORCHARD BOOKS

www.rainbowmagic.co.uk

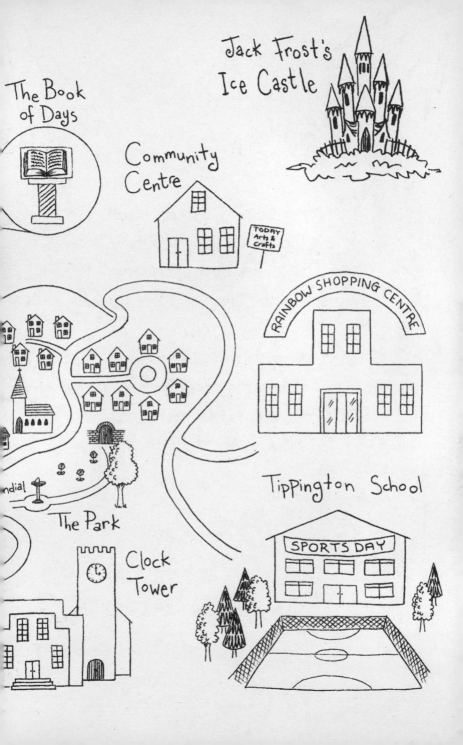

Icy wind now fiercely blow!
To the Time Tower I must go.
Goblin servants follow me
And steal the Fun Day Flags I need.

I know there will be no fun,
For fairies or humans once the flags are gone.
So, storm winds, take me where I say.
My plan for chaos starts today!

Contents

Fantastic Fashion

"You look gorgeous," Rachel Walker said, looking at her friend Kirsty Tate.

"So do you," Kirsty replied. The two girls grinned at each other. Kirsty was staying with Rachel for the half-term holiday and they'd been doing all sorts of fun things together. But today, Saturday, was going to be especially exciting.

Rachel's cousin, Caroline, was opening
a new boutique in the Rainbow Shopping
Centre, and was putting on a fashion
show featuring some of the boutique's
clothes. Even better, she had asked
Rachel and Kirsty to be two of her
catwalk models.

"There," said Anna, the stylist, as she

gave a last squirt
of hairspray to
Rachel's French
plait. "You
two are ready.
You'd better
find Caroline
and get your first
outfits on now.
The show starts in
fifteen minutes."

Kirsty and Rachel thanked Anna and clambered off their swivel seats. They were in the make-up room, which was part of the makeshift backstage area behind the catwalk.

Just then, Caroline appeared in the doorway. "Hi girls," she said. "You both look great. Let me show you around quickly before the show begins."

Kirsty and Rachel followed Caroline, both feeling tingly with excitement. The backstage area had been put together with large screens and partitions to make different rooms, and it was a bit of a maze. First, Caroline took them to see how the models would walk onto the catwalk. There were two concealed

entrances that led to a long, narrow stage
that had been set up in the large lobby of
the mall. Bright spotlights beamed down
on it, and a cameraman was setting up
his equipment.

"He's from the local press," Caroline told
the girls. "Hopefully we'll get a picture in
the *Gazette*. It would be brilliant publicity!"

Kirsty and Rachel could see that some people were already sitting in the rows of seats on either side of the catwalk. Unfortunately, none of them looked excited to be there. In fact, most of them appeared a little bored!

"The atmosphere feels rather flat," Caroline said, looking around with a puzzled expression. "Hopefully, once the rest of the audience arrive, everyone will feel a bit more excited."

Rachel shot Kirsty a look. Both girls knew exactly why the audience looked glum – it was because the Saturday Fun Flag was missing! Kirsty and Rachel were good friends with the fairies, and had been called to Fairyland many times to help out. This time, naughty Jack Frost had stolen the seven Fun Day Flags and taken them back to his ice castle. Without the flags, the Fun Day Fairies couldn't produce the special magic they needed to spread fun around the human world, and everyone was more miserable as a result. But Jack Frost's goblin servants had had so much fun with the Fun Day Flags around that they had grown mischievous and started playing pranks on Jack Frost himself.

Jack Frost eventually lost his temper
and banished the flags to the human
world. So far, Rachel and Kirsty had
helped the Fun Day Fairies find five of
their flags, but there were still two left
to find – including Saturday's!

"Now, the wardrobe room is just along

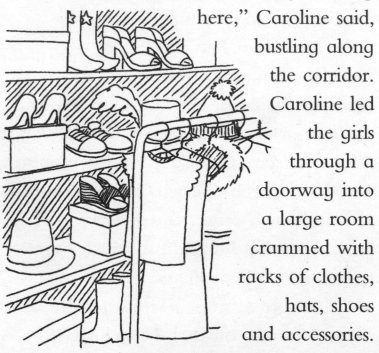

here," Caroline said,
bustling along
the corridor.
Caroline led
the girls
through a
doorway into
a large room
crammed with
racks of clothes,
hats, shoes
and accessories.

"Wow!" Rachel commented as she gazed around.

"You'll be wearing three outfits each," Caroline explained. "They're all here, with your names on them." She pulled out three hangers marked "Rachel" and three marked "Kirsty", then gave the girls boxes of shoes to match their outfits. "I'll leave you to get ready in here," she said, showing them into a small dressing room nearby.

She checked her watch. "You've got ten minutes to change into your first outfits before you're needed on stage."

Kirsty and Rachel hung up their clothes excitedly as Caroline rushed off. The first outfits they had to wear were party dresses with strappy shoes.

"This is lovely," Kirsty said, slipping into her long, silvery dress. "Will you zip me up please, Rachel?"

Rachel helped Kirsty, then put on a floaty pink dress and matching necklace. "This is going to be such fun even without the Fun Day Flag," she said, "but I hope we can find today's flag before any horrible goblins do!"

Rachel and Kirsty knew that they weren't the only ones looking for the Fun Day Flags. Jack Frost's goblins had so missed the fun the flags had brought to the ice castle that they had sneaked out, without their master's permission, to find them again.

"Girls, you look fabulous!" came
a voice from behind them.
Rachel and Kirsty
turned to see Susan,
Caroline's business
partner. "Come
to the catwalk
with me; you
two are first
on," she said,
smiling. "Try
and relax and
imagine you're at
a real party when

you're out there," she advised the girls
as she led them towards the catwalk.

Susan guided Rachel to the right
catwalk entrance and showed
Kirsty the entrance on the left. "When

I give you the cue, I want you to walk out of your entrances and meet in the middle," she said to them both. "Then you can walk down the main stage together. When you reach the end, you turn and walk back up and out through your stage entrances. Got that?"

Kirsty and Rachel just had time to nod and take up their places as the music started.

Susan winked at them. "You're on," she said. "Off you go!"

Fun on the Catwalk

Kirsty walked onto the stage, a little nervously. The lights were dazzling, but the music that was playing was her favourite song. She stepped forwards in time to the rhythm, and soon found herself grinning. This was fun!

But then Kirsty looked down at the spectators and nearly stumbled when she saw the gloomy expressions on some of their faces. Somebody had even fallen asleep!

Kirsty and Rachel walked towards each other and went the rest of the way down the catwalk together as Susan had instructed. "We've got to find the Saturday flag!" Rachel hissed out of the corner of her mouth. "Nobody's having any fun!"

Kirsty nodded. Rachel was right. They needed some fairy Fun Day Magic to put some sparkle into the show.

The girls had reached the end of the catwalk now, so they spun around and walked back the way they'd come. A feeble pattering of applause followed them. Once off stage, they exchanged worried glances.

"Where could the flag be?" Kirsty fretted as they returned to their changing room.

Rachel shook her head. "I don't know, but remember that the Fairy Queen always says we shouldn't look for the magic because it will come to us," she pointed out.

"I know," Kirsty said, gazing around the changing room. "I just hope it comes to us before the end of the fashion show, that's all!"

The next outfits that the girls had to wear were part of the boutique's winter collection. The girls had coats, boots, hats, gloves and scarves to put on over warm jumpers and trousers. Quickly, Kirsty pulled on her sweater and trousers and then took her coat off its hanger. As she did so, she let out a gasp. "Rachel, look!"

Rachel turned to see, and then she gasped, too. There was a bright pink scarf under Kirsty's coat, but it wasn't an ordinary scarf. It was fuchsia pink, with a sparkly sun pattern in the middle of it, and Rachel realised immediately that it was the Saturday Fun Flag.

"The magic did come to us!" Rachel declared, grinning. "Brilliant!"

Kirsty tied the flag carefully around her neck. "I'll keep it safe until we can find Sienna the Saturday Fairy," she said.

Rachel nodded. "And then she can take it back to Fairyland and recharge her wand." she agreed happily.

The girls knew that the Fun Day Flags served a very special purpose. Every morning in Fairyland, Francis the frog, the Royal Time Guard, went to the Time Tower to check which day it was in the Book of Days. He then selected the correct Fun Day Flag and ran it up the Time Tower flagpole, while that day's fairy waited below in the courtyard, her wand held high.

When the sun's rays shone onto the glittering flag, a stream of magical sparkles would be reflected from it and stream straight into the fairy's wand, charging the wand with special Fun Day Magic.

"The sooner Sienna recharges her wand, the sooner this audience will cheer up!" Kirsty added.

But then Rachel frowned. "You've got gloves, but I don't seem to have any," she said to Kirsty. "I wonder if I should have some too. I'll just go and check with Caroline."

Kirsty nodded and Rachel left her friend to finish getting dressed as she rushed out of the room.

"Oh, yes, you should have gloves," Caroline said, when Rachel found her. "Where could they have got to?" She started rummaging through the wardrobe room, trying to find them.

"Any luck?" Kirsty asked, appearing in the doorway a few minutes later. She had her full winter outfit on now. "Susan has just given me a two-minute warning until we're needed on the catwalk again," she added.

"Here they are!" Caroline said at last, pressing a pair of pale blue gloves into Rachel's hand.

"Thanks," Rachel said. "See you in a minute, Kirsty. I'll be as quick as I can!"

Rachel rushed back to the changing room, only to find that the rest of her outfit was missing now! She stared around in disbelief. Everything from her hat to her boots had completely vanished. "Oh, no!" she cried. "Where is everything?"

Just as the words left her mouth, a burst of bright pink sparkles suddenly streamed from one of the gloves in her hand and a tiny, smiling fairy peeped out.

Rachel recognised her immediately. "Sienna!" she exclaimed in relief. "I'm so glad to see you!"

Goblin Grab

Sienna the Saturday Fairy had long
brown hair tied in bunches, and wore
a red top with a pink pleated skirt.
A pink star necklace sparkled at her
throat, and she wore dainty red ballet
slippers on her feet. She beamed at
Rachel. "Sorry," she said, "I think it
was my fault that your gloves went

astray. I cast a spell so that I would
appear inside one of them, only I think
the magic made the gloves pop up in
a different place!"

"I'm just glad you're
here," Rachel assured
her. "Guess what?
Kirsty's found your
flag already!"

Sienna's eyes
shone with joy.
"I thought it
would be around
here somewhere
because of the
new poem in the
Book of Days this
morning," she said.
Then she recited aloud:

"Hats and scarves and coats and shoes,
The flag you'll find but then you'll lose.
Do not despair, remember this:
The fashion show is where it is!"

"Talking of the show," Rachel said anxiously, remembering what she was supposed to be doing. "I'm meant to be on stage, modelling, really soon, but my outfit's gone missing!"

"Don't worry," Sienna said, twirling her wand between her fingers. "If you tell me what you were supposed to be wearing, I can work some fairy magic for you."

Rachel smiled thankfully. "It was a thick white coat, with a fur-trimmed hood," she said, "a pale blue scarf and hat, and big white furry boots."

Sienna waved her wand at once and a flurry of pink sparkly fairy dust swirled around Rachel. Moments later, she was fully dressed in all the right clothes.

"Thank you Sienna. That's perfect!" Rachel laughed. "Now I'd better go."

Sienna nodded and hopped nimbly into Rachel's coat pocket as Rachel rushed out to the catwalk.

"OK, girls, you're on!" Rachel saw
Susan saying to Kirsty at the right
catwalk entrance, but when she looked
across to the left-hand
entrance, she stopped
in her tracks.
Standing there
was a different
model, and
whoever it was
was wearing
her outfit!

"Why would
anyone steal my
outfit and pretend to
be me?" she whispered to
Sienna, feeling confused. She peeped out
of the entrance as Kirsty and the other
model both set off down the catwalk.

She could see that the people in the
audience were starting to perk up
now, no doubt because the
Saturday flag was on
stage nearby. Kirsty
was smiling at them,
not realising that
it wasn't Rachel
who was
alongside her.

Rachel peered
closely at the
model who had
taken her place. As
she watched, she
saw that the model
had a very long, pointy,
green nose. "It's a goblin!"
she hissed in horror.

Sienna stared in disbelief. "A very tall goblin," she whispered anxiously. It was true. The goblin was at least twice as tall as he should have been. And now he was reaching a warty green hand towards the scarf around Kirsty's neck! "He's after the flag," Rachel cried in dismay. "We've got to stop him!" And she hurried out onto the catwalk, determined to warn Kirsty that there was a goblin on stage.

At the same moment, Kirsty reached
the end of the catwalk and did her twirl.
As she looked back down the way she
had come, she saw that there were two
Rachels, identically dressed, on stage
with her.

Kirsty gaped in surprise, and then her eyes narrowed as she realised that one of the Rachels was a goblin, but before she could react, the goblin lunged towards her. He snatched the Saturday Fun Flag from around her neck and pelted back along the catwalk.

Cloaked by Clothes

"Hey!" Rachel cried, seeing the goblin running down the catwalk towards her with the flag. She tried to stop him, but he tripped her up and poor Rachel went sprawling on her hands and knees. Kirsty ran over to help her up, but by that time the goblin had disappeared off the stage.

Rachel's cheeks were flushed. "Let's get off the catwalk so we can find that goblin," she said to Kirsty in a low voice, and together the friends marched quickly back down the catwalk. The audience were smiling and clapping – luckily, they seemed to think it was all part of the show!

Susan was waiting for the girls as they came off stage. "Are you all right?" she asked in concern. "I saw that you'd fallen, Rachel, but I didn't see how it happened. I was getting Emma ready," she explained, gesturing to another model who was now heading down the catwalk. "And then I looked around and saw you in a heap. Did you bump into each other?"

"Something like that," Rachel said. "But I'm fine now, don't worry."

"Glad to hear it," Susan said. "Take a few minutes to sit down and recover. I'll rearrange the order of the models for final outfits, so that you two are the last on. That way, you can get your breath back."

"Thanks, Susan," Kirsty said, but as soon as they were out of sight, she and Rachel looked at each other.

"There's no way we can sit down and have a rest now," Rachel said grimly.

"Not when we've a Fun Day Flag to get back," Kirsty agreed. "I can't believe that goblin just snatched it. I'm dreading having to tell Sienna."

"Don't worry,
Kirsty," Sienna
said, popping her
head out of
Rachel's pocket.
"I saw the whole
thing, and it
wasn't your fault."

Kirsty jumped at the
sound of Sienna's voice.
"Oh, hello, Sienna," she said, smiling
sheepishly. "I'm glad you're here, but
I'm sorry about your flag."

Sienna fluttered out of Rachel's pocket
and flew over to Kirsty. "It's all right,"
she said. "I guessed something like this
might happen after I read today's
poem." And then she recited it again for
Kirsty's benefit.

"Do not despair, remember this: the
fashion show is where it is," Kirsty
repeated thoughtfully when Sienna
had finished. "So the flag's still here
somewhere."

Sienna nodded.

"Look," Rachel said, as they went
past a pile of clothes on the floor.
"That's my outfit!"

"And a pair of stilts!" Sienna said,

pointing them
out to the girls.
"That's how the
goblin managed
to look so tall."
She waved her
wand, making the
pile of clothes and
the stilts vanish.

The girls and Sienna hurried on to the wardrobe room, and Rachel pushed the door open. "Let's start looking in here, shall we?" she suggested. "There are lots of places for a sneaky goblin to hide."

Kirsty and Sienna agreed, and the three friends crept into the room together. There were so many racks of clothes to search through that they each started looking in a different place.

Kirsty skimmed through a rack of long evening dresses — but there was nobody hiding between them. Sienna waved her wand, and a whole line of hats leapt off their pegs and up into the air, but there was nobody hiding underneath them.

Meanwhile, Rachel was flicking
through a rail of coats when she
suddenly spotted a pair of knobbly
green knees poking out from beneath
a toddler's yellow raincoat. When she
looked more closely, she could see
a corner of bright pink fabric showing,
too. It was the goblin and the Fun
Day Flag! Rachel crept towards him.

Goblin in a Spin

Just at that moment, the goblin peeped out from between the coats and saw Rachel coming towards him. With a cry of alarm, he darted away from her.

"I've found him; he's somewhere around here!" Rachel shouted to Sienna and Kirsty, and she squeezed through the coats to chase after the goblin.

Kirsty rushed over to help, and Sienna fluttered up into the air.

"I think I saw him in that corner," Sienna called to the girls, pointing with her wand.

"There he is!" cried Kirsty, spotting a large green ear poking out from behind a black dress. But once again, the goblin ducked away and ran off before the girls could reach him.

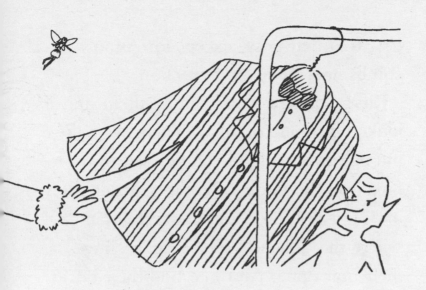

Rachel followed the sound of his footsteps and caught sight of his long nose sticking out of a man's suit. She made a lunge for him, but the goblin leapt away just before her fingers closed on the flag. This time he dashed right out of the room.

Kirsty and Rachel raced after him, with Sienna zooming alongside, as he ran into the make-up room.

It was empty now, except for Anna's combs and make-up collection.

Kirsty shut the door behind them and looked around carefully. There weren't many places to hide. There were no boxes on the floor, or cabinets to dodge into, just the three large swivel chairs where the girls had sat earlier to have their hair done. All three had their backs to the girls and Sienna.

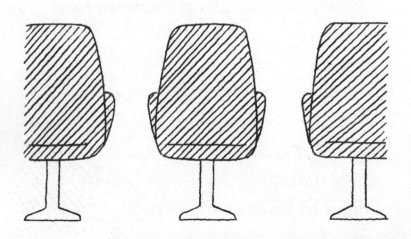

"He must be in one of those chairs," Kirsty mouthed to the others.

Rachel nodded thoughtfully. Then she took a deep breath, grabbed hold of the nearest chair to her and swung it around. *Whizz!* The chair spun around on its base, but it was empty.

Kirsty spun the second chair to face them, but that was empty, too. She and Rachel looked at each other. They both knew that the goblin had to be hiding in the third chair.

Kirsty grinned. "Sienna, could you use some fairy magic to spin that chair around really, really fast?" she whispered.

Sienna gave a low giggle, and nodded. She waved her wand at the third chair, and a flood of fuschia pink sparkles tumbled out from the tip. The chair immediately began to spin faster and faster and faster, until it was a blur in front of them. Now the girls could see that the goblin was indeed in the chair, and he was getting extremely dizzy!

"Stop! I feel sick," he moaned. "Let me off!"

Sienna waved her wand again, and the chair slowed and came to a stop. The goblin looked very pale as he clambered down from the chair. He swayed giddily, and then tried to run past the girls to the door. Unfortunately for the goblin, he was so dizzy he couldn't go in a straight line and he wobbled all over the place!

It was easy for Kirsty to grab the flag from his fingers. "I'll have that, thank you very much!" she cried triumphantly, holding the Saturday flag well out of the goblin's reach.

Saturday Fashion Fun!

Kirsty held out the flag to Sienna,
who waved her wand over it,
shrinking it to its usual Fairyland size.

"Thank you," Sienna beamed, and
then wagged a finger at the goblin.
"You're lucky I don't tell Jack Frost
what you've been up to!"

The goblin stuck his bottom lip out

in a sulky way and tried to storm off, but he was still so dizzy that he bumped into one of the make-up stands and sent everything flying! "*Atchoo!*" he sneezed, amidst clouds of face powder.

The girls couldn't help giggling as the goblin stomped away, dusty with powder and sneezing miserably.

"Well done, girls," Sienna said happily. She waved her wand over the spilled powder, and it promptly vanished. All of Anna's make-up brushes and pots bounced up from where they had scattered on the floor, and arranged themselves neatly back on the stand. The tub of face powder was instantly full again, and its lid jumped back on smartly. "That's better," Sienna said. She grinned at the girls. "And now you two should get dressed in your final outfits!"

"Oh, yes," Rachel cried, making for the door. "I'd almost forgotten about the show!"

Back in the little dressing room, the girls pulled on their outfits quickly. They wore sparkly tops with jeans and pretty pink and white trainers. Sienna helpfully waved her wand to tie the laces in the trainers as the girls put them on.

"Thanks, Sienna." Kirsty smiled, tidying her hair in the mirror.

"Good luck," Sienna replied. "I'll go back to Fairyland now to charge up my wand. Hopefully, I'll be back with some Saturday Fun Day magic very soon!"

Kirsty and Rachel
ran to the catwalk,
and Susan and
Caroline checked
their outfits
before they
went on.

"You look
wonderful,"
Caroline told them.

"Everyone's been
great," Susan added,
smiling at some of the other models
nearby. "In fact, the whole show has
been great!" Then the smile slipped from
her face. "I just can't understand why
the audience isn't having a better time."

Caroline nodded. "It is a bit
disappointing," she admitted.

Rachel felt sorry for her cousin. She and Susan had clearly worked so hard to get the whole fashion show together. "Hopefully, they'll love these last outfits," she said with a big smile. "I know I do."

Caroline hugged her. "Thanks, Rachel," she said. "Now you two had better get ready. You're on next!"

Kirsty and Rachel went to their entrances and stepped onto the stage when Susan gave them their cue.

A party tune started up, and a pink
spotlight suddenly shone on
a huge sparkly disco ball
above the catwalk. The
glitter ball started
spinning around,
sending tiny
colourful spots of
light all over
the audience.
"Oooh!" people
said in delight,
and Kirsty and
Rachel couldn't
help smiling at
each other. This
was more like it!
"This is Sienna's magic,
I bet," Rachel said happily.

The girls began dancing along the catwalk, and then Susan and Caroline ushered all the other models onto the catwalk too, to dance along behind them. It wasn't long before the audience were up on their feet, dancing and clapping, and having a brilliant time.

"All of a sudden, this feels like a party!" Kirsty cheered to Rachel.

"Yes, thanks to you-know-who!" Rachel replied. The girls glanced up to see Sienna riding on the twirling glitter ball and waving merrily at them. Then the little fairy blew them a kiss and waved her wand over the whole mall. There was a loud pop, and then glittery confetti and streamers, in all the colours of the rainbow, showered down from the ceiling over everyone.

A great cheer went up from the models and audience alike. Everyone was having a fabulous, glittery time and the *Gazette* photographer was taking lots of photos.

Sienna fluttered down, camouflaged within the confetti, to say a last goodbye. "Thanks again, girls," she said to Rachel and Kirsty. "I must go and carry on my Fun Day work. Enjoy yourselves, and goodbye!"

"Everyone's having great fun now thanks to you!" Kirsty said, smiling.

"Yes, thanks Sienna," Rachel agreed. "Goodbye!"

Sienna waved and disappeared in a whirl of pink sparkles.

The music ended a few minutes later, and the audience gave Caroline, Susan and the models a standing ovation.

Rachel couldn't stop beaming. "The fashion show was a massive success," she whispered to Kirsty.

Kirsty nodded. "And now there's only one flag left to find!" she added happily.

Win Rainbow Magic Goodies!

There are lots of Rainbow Magic fairies, and we want to know which one is your favourite! Send us a picture of her and tell us in thirty words why she is your favourite and why you like Rainbow Magic books. Each month we will put the entries into a draw and select one winner to receive a Rainbow Magic Sparkly T-shirt and Goody Bag!

Send your entry on a postcard to Rainbow Magic Competition, Orchard Books, 338 Euston Road, London NW1 3BH. Australian readers should email: childrens.books@hachette.com.au New Zealand readers should write to Rainbow Magic Competition, 4 Whetu Place, Mairangi Bay, Auckland NZ. Don't forget to include your name and address. Only one entry per child.

Good luck!

The Fun Day Fairies

Megan, Talullah, Willow, Thea, Freya
and Sienna have got their flags back.
Now Rachel and Kirsty must help

Sarah the Sunday Fairy

Gobbling Goblin

"I can't believe it's Sunday already!"
Kirsty Tate said, glancing at her best
friend Rachel Walker. They were in the
Walkers' kitchen, wrapping sandwiches in
plastic bags. "And Mum and Dad are
coming to fetch me tonight," Kirsty
added. "Hasn't this week gone quickly?"

"Yes, it has," Rachel agreed. "That's
because we've been busy looking for the
fairies' Fun Day Flags!"

Just then Mr Walker hurried in,
carrying a large wicker picnic basket.
Rachel stopped talking immediately and
grinned at Kirsty. Nobody else knew that

the two girls had a magical secret:
they were friends with the fairies!

For the last week the two girls had
been trying to find the missing Fun
Day Flags and return them to the
seven Fun Day Fairies. The flags were
very important because the fairies used
their magic to make every day of the
week fun. Naughty Jack Frost and his
goblin servants had stolen the flags, but
the flags' special magic meant that the
goblins had fun all the time instead of
working. Jack Frost had become so
annoyed that he cast a spell and
banished the flags to the human world.
However, his cheeky goblin servants
had missed having fun so much that,
unknown to Jack Frost, they had
sneaked away to try and get the
flags back...

Have you checked out the

RAINBOW magic®

website at:

www.rainbowmagic.co.uk